Carla's Breakfast

written by
Leslie Harper

illustrated by
Paul Drzewiecki

"I've made you a bowl of hot oatmeal for breakfast," called Mom.

"I don't want oatmeal," said Carla.
"May I have the cereal with the
red, yellow and green dots in
a bowl of cold milk?"

"We don't have any," called Mom.
"Please come and eat your oatmeal."

"I don't want oatmeal," said Carla. "May I have the cereal with plump juicy raisins in a bowl of cold milk?"

"We don't have any," called Mom.
"Please come and eat your oatmeal."

"I don't want oatmeal," said Carla.
"May I have the cereal that's brown
and round in a bowl of cold milk?"

"We don't have any," called Mom. "Please come and eat your oatmeal, dear."

"I don't want oatmeal," said Carla.
"May I have the cereal that you
munch and crunch in a
bowl of cold milk?"

"We don't have any," called Mom. "Please come and eat your oatmeal, Carla."

"I don't want oatmeal," said Carla.
"May I have the cereal with nuts and
honey in a bowl of cold milk?"

"We don't have any," called Mom.
"Please come and eat your
oatmeal, now!"

"I don't want oatmeal," said Carla.
"May I have the cereal with the
A B C's in a bowl of cold milk?"

"We don't have any," said Mom.

"Please! Eat your oatmeal."

"But Mom, my oatmeal is cold
and the bus is here!"